ABUELITA AND me

words by
Leonarda Carranza

pictures by
Rafael Mayani

annick
press
toronto • berkeley

Every day it's just Abuelita and me.

And inside, we have so much fun together.

Inside, we spend hours drawing pictures of monsters.
Abuelita tries her hardest, but my monsters are the scariest!

Inside, I paint my nails and Abuelita's.
I like to paint her nails pink and purple.
Abuelita doesn't mind that I accidentally paint her fingers.

Inside, we can be silly.

We flap our arms like birds,
so our nails dry before we go outside.

I like going outside, too, but sometimes people are not nice to Abuelita. They don't know or they forget that Abuelita is the best grandma in the world.

Sometimes when Abuelita speaks, they pretend she's invisible.

Sometimes they get up and move away when she sits next to them.

Sometimes they make mean faces when they see her.

No matter what happens outside, Abuelita always smiles and says, "It's okay, Amorcito."

Today, Abuelita winks at me because we're making her special sopa so it's worth it to go outside. I rush to get ready.

At the store, we find almost everything we're looking for to make Abuelita's special soup—everything except yuca.

Abuelita asks the grocery clerk if he knows where we can find it, but he says, "What? What? Huh? What did you say?"

And Abuelita keeps trying to ask for yuca, and she uses both its names, yuca and cassava, but the man gets tired of listening and swats her away like she's a mosquito.

We circle and circle the aisles,
but we don't find yuca.

I feel tired by the time we're outside
waiting for the bus to take us home.

On the bench, I ask Abuelita why grown-ups
don't understand her if they're big, but I
understand everything, and I'm still small.

But Abuelita says, "Don't worry about that, Amorcito."

Sometimes I want to show grown-ups how to listen.
It's not too hard to hear what Abuelita is saying.

When the bus comes, Abuelita tells the driver, "One moment, please," and we find two seats in the middle section so Abuelita can go through her purse.

But the driver stops the bus.

Instead of asking, *what, what, huh,* he stomps towards us.

"You have to pay," he says.

Abuelita is taking so long to find the change, and now the bus driver is so close that I have to look down at my hands.

"I won't start the bus until you pay," he shouts.
"You people are always trying to get away with something.
Do you understand me? You have to pay!"

I want to explain that Abuelita would never steal, that she's afraid of falling because last winter, she fell on the ice, and she needs to sit down.

But the bus driver is yelling, so instead of helping, I start to cry.
Finally, Abuelita finds the right change and hands it to the driver.
He marches to the front and starts the bus again.

Abuelita hugs me and says, "Shhhh, it's okay, Amorcito."

But it's not okay. I look around the bus,
and no one wants to look at us.

I feel so small, like we are shrinking.
Like it's just Abuelita and me all alone in the world.

The next day, Abuelita comes into my room with
my pancakes and asks if I want to go to the library.
I say no. I want to stay in bed.

In the afternoon, Abuelita asks if I want
to get ice cream and go to the park.
I shake my head.

A few hours later, it's raining, and Abuelita takes out our rain boots.

"Do you want to go splashing in the rain?" she says.

Abuelita says, "Por favor, we've been inside all day, Amorcito."

I start to cry. Abuelita hugs me and says, "It's okay to be sad. I'm sad, too. We can stay inside today, but maybe we can look for yuca tomorrow?"

I turn to Abuelita and shout, "Do you want to get yelled at again?"

And Abuelita says, "Cariño, we didn't do anything wrong."
She holds my face in her hands and kisses me.
"What happened is not our fault.
We are not the ones that need to hide."

It doesn't make any sense. Abuelita used to know everything, but now she knows nothing.

I stay in my room, and I wonder how we're going to get groceries if we can't go outside again.

In the morning, I walk slowly to the kitchen. I think Abuelita is going to be mad. I think she is going to say, "Hurry up. We need to get to the store."

But Abuelita isn't mad.

She doesn't say, "You're being impossible," or "You're such a baby." Instead, Abuelita smiles.

We don't talk about the bus or groceries.

After breakfast, we have fun inside and outside.

First, I help pull weeds in the garden. When it starts to rain, I say, "Please can we go for a walk?" And so we put on our raincoats and rain boots and go splashing.

My splashes are the biggest. Abuelita tries, too, so I tell her that her splashes are big, even though they're so small.

And Abuelita doesn't say anything.
She doesn't have to.

She is smiling so big all her teeth are showing,
and I'm smiling so much, too. I can't stop.

We walk to the middle section, and we sit down. It takes him a bit, but the driver starts the bus and keeps driving.

And I'm so proud of us.

I take the change from Abuelita's hand, and when the bus doors open, I march in and put the money in the fare box. I'm scared. I try not to look right at him, but I see him. It's the same driver.

"That better be enough!" he says, and I'm too busy trying not to see his angry face that I can't think of what to say.

Abuelita stands beside me.

"It is enough," she says. "It's enough."

When I see the bus in the distance, I squeeze Abuelita's hand so tight.
I want to go home.

Abuelita kneels beside me. She says,
"Amorcito, we don't need to do this right now."

But then the anger bubbles in my belly.
I can't go home.

The next day, after I finish my pancakes, I tell Abuelita that I'm ready to go back on the bus. Even though I'm not ready. Not really really ready.

Abuelita says, "Cariño, there is no rush."

But I don't want to keep waiting.

I tell Abuelita, "I AM READY. I AM READY. Don't you believe me?"

But then at night, in my bed, my sadness grows.

Then I feel angry.

I don't want to think about Abuelita being sad about the bus.

We spend the night drawing
more monsters. This time,
I draw monsters driving busses.

When I show Abuelita,
she looks sad.

I don't want to make Abuelita sad, so I tear up one of
my monsters. "He's not stronger than me," I tell her.

I give her one of the pictures so she can tear it, too.
But Abuelita doesn't want to. She puts it back on the
table and instead, she tries to smile.

And it feels like it's just the two of us in the whole world.

To Kika, Abuelita, Grandma, and all
the generous, loving, and fierce abuelitas.
— L. C.

A mis Abuelitas, Nelly y Conchita.
— R. M.

Cover art by Rafael Mayani, designed by Paul Covello
Interior designed by Paul Covello
Edited by Claire Caldwell

Annick Press Ltd.

We acknowledge the support of the Canada Council for the Arts and the Ontario Arts Council, and the participation of the
Government of Canada/la participation du gouvernement du Canada for our publishing activities.

Library and Archives Canada Cataloguing in Publication

Title: Abuelita and me / words by Leonarda Carranza ; pictures by Rafael Mayani.
Names: Carranza, Leonarda, author. | Mayani, Rafael, illustrator.
Identifiers: Canadiana (print) 20210330988 | Canadiana (ebook) 20210330996 | ISBN 9781773216102
   (hardcover) | ISBN 9781773216119 (HTML) | ISBN 9781773216126 (PDF)
Classification: LCC PS8605.A7735 A63 2022 | DDC jC813/.6—dc23

Published in the U.S.A. by Annick Press (U.S.) Ltd.
Distributed in Canada by University of Toronto Press.
Distributed in the U.S.A. by Publishers Group West.

Printed in China

annickpress.com
leonardacarranza.com
rafaelmayani.com

Spanish edition available 978-1-77321-659-1
Also available as an e-book. Please visit annickpress.com/ebooks for more details.